ROYAL REEDS

House Mates

Reverse Harem Romance Book Two

Contents

Chapter 1

Luna Blake sat at her desk, staring blankly at the spreadsheet on her laptop, her mind a thousand miles away. The hum of the office buzzed around her, phones ringing, the tapping of keyboards, and the soft murmur of her coworkers engaged in conversations she had no interest in. The suffocating feeling had been building for weeks now, a heavy weight pressing down on her chest. The deadlines, the constant pressure from clients, and the endless meetings were all too much. She needed to get out.

When her best friend, Jenna, had suggested a weekend ski trip, Luna had been reluctant at first. She wasn't exactly the outdoorsy type. She preferred the controlled chaos of the city, the hustle and bustle of streets lined with coffee shops and skyscrapers, not wide-open spaces and snow-covered mountains. But Jenna had been persistent.

"You need this," she had said, her tone filled with certainty. "Fresh mountain air, a hot tub, and a few glasses of wine. Trust me."

And so, here she was, driving up winding mountain roads, wondering if she'd made the right decision. The landscape was breathtaking—pine trees dusted with snow lined the roads, and the towering peaks of the mountains loomed in the distance, their jagged edges softened by the blanket of white. Luna had to admit, it was beautiful. Peaceful, even.

After a few hours, she finally arrived at the small ski town Jenna had booked for them. It was like something out of a postcard—quaint cabins with smoke curling out of chimneys, twinkling fairy lights hanging from the rooftops, and the smell of pine in the crisp air. It was hard not to be charmed by the place.

Luna checked into the lodge, dropped off her bags, and met up with her friends for a quick lunch. The cozy warmth of the lodge and the laughter of her friends started to chip away at her stress, and for the first time in what felt like forever, she began to relax.

The next morning, they hit the slopes.

Luna had hoped skiing would be intuitive, but after an hour of struggling to stay upright on the slippery sticks strapped to her feet, she was over it. Her friends were laughing and gliding down the mountain with ease while she wobbled awkwardly behind them.

It wasn't long before she took her first fall. Then her second. And her third.

With snow stuck to her face and bruises forming on her body, she felt utterly defeated. Skiing, it turned out, was not her forte.

"Maybe you should take a break," Jenna said, gliding over with an amused smile. "I'll join you in a bit. Just don't give up yet."

It was too late. Luna had already made up her mind. She was done. Embarrassed and sore, she forced a smile, gave a quick nod, and told her friends she'd meet them later. She just needed some quiet time, a break from the chaos on the slopes.

She returned to the lodge, intending to curl up by the fire with a book, but as she passed through the crowded lodge, filled with laughter and activity, she felt restless again. The idea of sitting inside didn't appeal to her. She needed to escape.

Grabbing her keys, Luna decided to take a drive. Maybe she could explore the town a bit or find a more secluded spot to enjoy the scenery in peace. She bundled up, slipped into her car, and drove away from the lodge, following a winding road that led deeper into the mountains.

As she drove, the air seemed to grow colder, and the once-gentle snowfall began to thicken, falling in heavy, swirling flakes that blurred her vision. She hadn't realized a storm was coming in until it was too late. The snow quickly turned into a blizzard, the wind howling and shaking her car as it struggled to maintain traction on the slick, icy road.

Luna's heart pounded in her chest as she gripped the steering wheel, trying to stay calm. She had never driven in conditions like this before, and the panic started to creep in.

Suddenly, her tires hit a patch of ice, and the car skidded out of control. She cried out in surprise, her hands jerking the wheel as the car spun off the road and slid down a small embankment, coming to a sudden stop against a snowdrift.

For a moment, Luna just sat there, her breath coming in short, shallow gasps. The storm raged outside, and the interior of the car was already growing colder. She couldn't stay here—she had to find help, but where?

With trembling hands, she pulled out her phone, hoping for a signal, but there was none. The storm had knocked out any chance of communication. The panic she'd been holding at bay started to rise, but she forced herself to breathe deeply. There had to be something nearby—a cabin, a ranger station, anything.

Bundling up in her coat and scarf, Luna grabbed her small backpack, stuffed it with essentials—her phone, water, a flashlight—and pushed open the car door. The cold hit her like a punch to the gut, the icy wind stinging her face as she stumbled out into the snow. The storm was blinding, the snow so thick she could barely see more than a few feet ahead.

But then, through the swirling white, she spotted something—a faint glow in the distance. A cabin.

Relief washed over her as she trudged through the snow, her legs burning with the effort. The wind whipped around her, threatening to knock her off balance, but she kept her eyes fixed on the light ahead. It was her only hope.

When she finally reached the cabin, she banged on the door, her knuckles numb from the cold. She waited, breathless, her body trembling from both the cold and the adrenaline.

A few seconds later, the door swung open, and Luna blinked against the sudden warmth that spilled out.

Standing in the doorway was a man, tall and broad-shouldered, with dark hair tousled from sleep and a strong jawline set in a look of surprise. His piercing eyes swept over her, taking in her disheveled appearance.

"Are you okay?" he asked, his voice deep and gravelly.

"I—I got stranded. My car slid off the road," Luna stammered, her teeth chattering uncontrollably. "Please, I just need to warm up."

Without hesitation, the man reached for her, gently pulling her inside and closing the door behind her, shutting out the storm. The warmth of the cabin enveloped her like a blanket, but it did little to stop the uncontrollable shaking of her body.

"Logan, who's at the door?" Came a voice from the other side of the room. Another man appeared, this one blonde and slightly taller, with a grin that could melt ice. His eyes sparkled with amusement as he took in the situation.

"Well, well, looks like we've got a visitor."

The first man, Logan, shot him a look of mild annoyance before turning back to Luna. "You're lucky you found this place," he said, his tone softening. "The storm's only getting worse. You can stay here until it passes."

Luna nodded, still too shaken to speak. She had no idea what she had just stumbled into, but as she stood there, warming her frozen hands by the fire, she couldn't shake the feeling that her life had just taken an unexpected turn.

Chapter 2

Luna sank into the soft leather armchair by the fire, letting its warmth thaw her frozen limbs. The smell of pine and burning wood filled the cabin, and the crackling fire was the only sound competing with the howling wind outside. For a moment, she allowed herself to relax, closing her eyes and focusing on the heat slowly seeping back into her body.

When she opened them, Logan was standing near the kitchen, pouring hot water into a mug. His dark hair was still slightly tousled, but there was an alertness in his movements now. His chiseled jaw was set in concentration, though his eyes flicked to her occasionally with a mixture of curiosity and concern.

The other man, Kai, leaned casually against the mantel, watching her with an easy grin that reached his blue eyes. Where Logan was all brooding intensity, Kai was the complete opposite—lighthearted and playful, with a confidence that came naturally.

"Well, it looks like we're going to be spending some quality time together," Kai said, his voice low and teasing. "This storm isn't going anywhere for days. You picked quite the night to go for a drive."

Luna forced a small smile, though the realization of her situation started to settle in. Snowed in, in a cabin with two complete strangers—handsome strangers, no less. The flicker of tension in the air was unmistakable, and she couldn't quite tell if it was nerves or something else stirring inside her.

"Here," Logan said, walking over with a steaming mug. His voice was softer now, the edge of irritation gone. He handed her the drink, and as their fingers brushed, a small spark jolted through her. She quickly wrapped her hands around the cup, grateful for the distraction.

"Thank you," she murmured, taking a sip. The warmth spread through her instantly, though it did little to ease the tension she felt sitting between them.

"No signal out here, I'm afraid," Kai said, walking over to sit on the couch across from her. "You're stuck with us for a bit. Hope you don't mind."

Luna glanced between them, unsure of how to respond. Being stuck in a snowstorm wasn't exactly her idea of a relaxing weekend, but she couldn't deny there was something oddly thrilling about it too. The two men radiated a quiet confidence, and their undeniable good looks didn't make things any easier. She had to remind herself that this was just a temporary situation—she needed to stay focused on getting through the storm, not on how they both seemed to fill the room with their presence.

"No, it's fine," she said finally, her voice sounding steadier than she felt. "I'm just thankful you were here. I wasn't sure how much longer I could have stayed out there in the cold."

Logan nodded, his intense gaze holding hers for a beat too long. "It's dangerous to be driving in weather like this. You were lucky."

Kai chuckled, leaning back on the couch with a casual ease that made Luna both nervous and intrigued. "Lucky to find us, at least," he said with a wink.

"I'd say the storm's already working in your favor."

Luna smiled awkwardly, unsure of how to respond to his flirtatious tone, but as the silence stretched between them, the heat of the fire started to feel suffocating, and not because of the temperature. There was something electric in the air, something unspoken but very present.

Logan moved back to the fire, grabbing a couple of logs and placing them on the flames. His strong, capable hands worked with precision, and for a moment, Luna couldn't tear her eyes away. He was quiet, focused, and there was something about his presence that both calmed and unsettled her. The contrast between the two men—Logan's intense quietness and Kai's easy charm—kept her on edge.

"So," Kai said, breaking the silence, "What's a city girl like you doing out here, anyway? Not exactly prime conditions for sightseeing."

Luna hesitated, unsure how much to reveal. She didn't want to seem vulnerable, but at the same time, these men were strangers.

"I was here on a ski trip with some friends," she explained. "I'm not much of a skier, though. I ended up leaving the lodge early and didn't realize how bad the storm was getting."

Kai raised an eyebrow, his grin widening. "Not much of a skier? Guess you're not the outdoorsy type then, huh?"

Luna bristled slightly at his teasing but quickly shrugged it off. "Not really. I like the idea of it, but the reality is… well, different."

Logan glanced over at her, his eyes lingering just a moment too long. "You could've gotten seriously hurt out there. It's good you found us when you did."

The weight of his words settled over her, and Luna felt the unspoken intensity behind them. There was something protective about Logan's demeanor, though he didn't say much. It was clear he took the storm seriously, and it made her feel oddly safe despite the unfamiliarity of the situation.

"Guess I'll have to improve my survival skills," Luna said, attempting to lighten the mood. But the tension between them remained thick, a quiet awareness of their shared isolation.

Kai leaned forward, his grin never faltering. "Don't worry, we've got plenty of survival skills between the two of us. You're in good hands."

Luna's cheeks flushed at the double meaning in his words, and she quickly took another sip of her drink, trying to hide the reaction. The firelight flickered across Kai's face, casting his features in a warm glow. He was undeniably handsome, with an effortless charm that drew her in, but then there was Logan—silent, brooding, and every bit as magnetic in his own way. She found herself pulled between them, unsure of how to navigate the growing tension.

As the hours passed, the wind outside howled louder, the snow piling up against the windows. The storm showed no signs of letting up, and the realization that they would be stuck together for days began to sink in.

Kai excused himself to the kitchen, leaving Luna and Logan in the quiet cabin. The crackling fire was the only sound, and Luna felt the weight of Logan's presence beside her.

"You should get some rest," Logan said, his voice low and rough. "It's going to be a long night."

Luna glanced up at him, her heart beating a little faster under his gaze. There was something about Logan that made her feel like she was under a microscope, like he could see right through her. But instead of feeling exposed, it only deepened her curiosity about him.

"I don't think I could sleep right now," she admitted, trying to sound casual.

Logan's eyes held hers, and for a moment, the air between them seemed to thicken with something unsaid. His jaw tightened slightly, as if he were holding back something. Then he stood, breaking the moment.

"Suit yourself," He said, his voice rough as he stepped away from her and headed toward the back of the cabin.

Luna watched him go, her pulse still racing. As the door to the back room closed behind him, she leaned back in the chair, exhaling a shaky breath. She was in for an interesting few days, and the realization hit her hard.

Two men, one cabin, and no way out.

Chapter 3

The evening settled in around them like a heavy blanket, the storm outside continuing to rage with no sign of stopping. Luna sat curled up on the couch, feeling the comforting warmth of the fire against her skin, though she was far from relaxed. The tension between her and the two men was palpable, an unspoken energy that buzzed in the air every time their eyes met.

Logan was seated in the large armchair by the fire, a book resting in his hands. His sharp, angular features were softened by the flickering light, but the intensity in his dark eyes remained. He didn't speak much—he didn't need to. Every now and then, he'd glance up from his book, his gaze locking with Luna's for a moment too long, sending a jolt of heat through her. It was those quiet, smoldering looks that made her pulse quicken. There was something about Logan—something unspoken and brooding that both intrigued and unsettled her.

He caught her watching him at one point and raised an eyebrow, the hint of a smile tugging at his lips. "Enjoying the view?" He asked, his voice low and teasing.

Luna flushed, quickly looking away. "Just wondering what you're reading."

Logan's smile deepened, though he didn't answer right away. Instead, he leaned back in his chair, his gaze still fixed on her. "It's not the book you're interested in, is it?"

His tone sent shivers down her spine, and she found herself at a loss for words. Logan's teasing was rare, but when it came, it was like a slow burn, laced with a quiet intensity that left her breathless. She quickly turned her attention to Kai, hoping for a distraction.

Kai was the complete opposite of Logan—open, playful, and utterly unbothered by the storm. He moved around the small kitchen, preparing dinner with a casual ease that made it seem like they were just three friends spending a normal evening together. His laughter filled the cabin as he chopped vegetables, throwing playful comments over his shoulder.

"So, Luna," Kai called out, glancing at her with a grin. "Do you cook, or are you more of a takeout kind of girl?"

Luna chuckled, grateful for the lighthearted change in conversation. "Takeout, definitely. I'd probably burn down my kitchen if I tried cooking half the things you're doing over there."

Kai laughed, the sound warm and infectious. "Lucky for you, I'm a pretty decent cook. Looks like you won't have to rely on your survival skills just yet."

Luna couldn't help but smile at his easygoing nature. Kai made everything seem effortless, and his constant stream of jokes helped ease the tension that had been building since she arrived. He had that rare ability to make anyone feel at home, and despite the strange circumstances, she found herself relaxing in his presence.

As Kai worked on dinner, he and Luna chatted about everything and nothing—

her job in the city, his life as a ski instructor, and how he ended up here in this remote mountain town. He was quick to smile, his blue eyes twinkling with mischief, and Luna found herself laughing more than she had in months.

"You must get a lot of women asking for private lessons," Luna teased, raising an eyebrow as Kai leaned against the counter with a smirk.

Kai chuckled, shrugging. "What can I say? It's part of the job. Although, I'm pretty selective about who I teach."

Luna rolled her eyes, though she couldn't deny how easy it was to flirt with him. "Oh, I bet you are."

Kai grinned, his gaze lingering on her in a way that made her heart skip a beat. "Don't worry, Luna. I'll give you a private lesson anytime you want."

The playful banter between them was intoxicating, and Luna found herself drawn to Kai's lighthearted charm. He was the kind of guy who could turn any situation into fun, and in the middle of a snowstorm, that was exactly what she needed. Even as she laughed with Kai, she was acutely aware of Logan's presence across the room, watching their exchange with those dark, brooding eyes.

After a while, Logan closed his book with a soft thud and leaned forward, resting his elbows on his knees. "Kai, you're not going to make her do all the work, are you?" He said, his voice teasing but edged with something deeper.

Kai smirked, glancing back at Logan. "I'm handling it, Logan. Maybe you should put down your book and help out."

Logan's lips twitched into a half-smile, but his eyes never left Luna's. "I'm sure Luna would appreciate a real meal, not whatever quick-fix nonsense you're putting together."

Luna felt her pulse quicken under the weight of his gaze, and the easy atmosphere that Kai had created suddenly shifted. Logan had a way of turning everything serious, making every word feel like it carried more meaning than it should.

"Trust me," Kai replied with a wink at Luna. "She's going to love it."

By the time dinner was ready, the tension in the room had shifted yet again. Kai's lighthearted energy clashed with Logan's quiet intensity, and Luna found herself caught in the middle, drawn to both men in different ways. Kai's charm made her feel at ease, like they'd been friends forever, but Logan… Logan made her heart race with a single look, his presence a constant reminder of something unspoken between them.

They sat down together at the small dining table, and the conversation continued. Kai kept things light, filling the silence with stories about the town and their life as ski instructors, but every now and then, Luna would catch Logan watching her, his dark eyes reflecting the flickering firelight.

"So, Luna," Kai said as they finished their meal, his grin returning. "You've told us a lot about work, but what do you do for fun?"

Luna paused, caught off guard by the question. Fun. It felt like such a foreign concept lately, with her job consuming so much of her time and energy.

"I don't know," she admitted, glancing down at her hands. "I used to read a lot, go out with friends, but lately, it's been all work. That's why I came on this trip, I guess. I needed to get away."

Kai's smile softened, his teasing tone fading. "Everyone needs a break sometimes. Maybe this storm's a blessing in disguise."

Logan, who had been silent for most of the meal, spoke up then. "Maybe it's a reminder," He said, his voice low. "That sometimes you have to stop running and face what's really bothering you."

Luna looked up, her heart skipping a beat at the intensity in his gaze. There was something in his words that hit too close to home, something that made her feel exposed in a way she hadn't expected. Logan wasn't the type to make idle conversation—every word seemed to carry weight, and she had the sense that he could see through the facade she tried to maintain.

For a moment, the air between them was thick with tension, and Luna found herself unable to look away from Logan's smoldering gaze. Before she could respond, Kai clapped his hands together, breaking the spell.

"Well, I think that's enough serious talk for one night," He said with a grin. "How about a little after-dinner drink? We've got some whiskey around here somewhere."

Luna laughed softly, grateful for the distraction. As Kai moved to the kitchen to grab the bottle, she leaned back in her chair, her mind racing. The storm outside may have trapped her in this cabin, but it was the storm brewing inside—between her, Kai, and Logan—that truly had her on edge.

Chapter 4

The snow continued to batter the cabin, the storm outside showing no sign of stopping, but inside, the fire crackled warmly, casting soft shadows across the room. The evening had drifted into night, and as the whiskey bottle on the table slowly emptied, so did Luna's lingering worries about the outside world. The storm, her car, the city—all of it faded away as she sat between Logan and Kai, feeling the strange tension that had been building throughout the night.

It started innocently enough. After dinner, the three of them had moved back to the cozy living area, sharing stories over glasses of wine and whiskey. Luna found herself laughing more than she had in months, swept up in Kai's infectious energy as he regaled them with hilarious tales of the eccentric tourists they dealt with on the slopes. Logan, in contrast, was quieter, but every now and then he would offer a dry remark that sent a ripple of amusement through the room. It was a different kind of humor—subtle, but no less effective.

Luna couldn't deny it any longer: she was drawn to both of them, in very different ways. Kai's flirtatious nature was undeniable, his easy charm making her feel instantly comfortable. He had a way of making her forget the awkwardness of their situation, as if being snowed in with two strangers was just an adventure waiting to unfold. His hand would sometimes brush against hers as he passed the bottle, sending little sparks of warmth through her that had nothing to do with the fire.

Then there was Logan.

Logan, who sat closer to the fire, his gaze occasionally flickering toward her with a heat that felt almost tangible. He wasn't as overt as Kai, but there was something about him that made her pulse race. Every time their eyes met, it was as though an unspoken understanding passed between them—something simmering just beneath the surface, waiting for the right moment to break free.

As the night wore on, the boundaries between them blurred. The alcohol softened her inhibitions, and with every passing story, every shared laugh, Luna felt the distance between them shrinking. At one point, she realized she was leaning closer to Logan, her arm brushing his as she shifted in her seat. She glanced at him, expecting him to move away, but instead, his dark eyes met hers, and for a split second, everything else in the room faded away. The pull between them was undeniable.

Kai's laughter broke the moment, and Luna blinked, quickly shifting her attention back to him. He was leaning against the armrest of the couch, a mischievous grin playing on his lips as he handed her another glass of wine.

"You know," Kai said, his voice low and teasing, "For someone who claims not to be much of an outdoorsy girl, you're handling this whole snowstorm thing pretty well."

Luna laughed, feeling the warmth of the wine settle into her veins. "I guess I'm full of surprises."

Kai raised an eyebrow, his grin widening. "I'm beginning to think so."

The flirtation was easy with Kai. It was light, playful, and didn't carry the weight that seemed to hang in the air whenever Logan was involved. But that didn't mean the attraction wasn't real. Sitting between the two men, Luna felt the unfamiliar pull growing stronger. She had never been in a situation like this before—drawn to two men at the same time, both of them so different yet equally magnetic. It was thrilling, and terrifying, and completely confusing.

As if sensing her thoughts, Logan's voice cut through the comfortable silence. "So, Luna," he said, his tone quiet but filled with that same slow-burning intensity, "What do you really want out of this weekend?"

The question caught her off guard, and for a moment, she didn't know how to answer. What *did* she want? She had come here to escape, to get away from the pressures of her job and the suffocating routine of her life in the city, but now, here, in this cabin with Logan and Kai, everything she thought she wanted seemed to shift.

"I don't know," she said honestly, her voice softer than she intended. "I just… needed a break, I guess. To clear my head."

Logan's gaze didn't waver, and Luna felt the weight of his attention fully on her. "And are you getting that?"

There was something about the way he asked the question, as if he was probing deeper than just her need for a vacation. Luna swallowed, feeling her pulse quicken under his steady stare. She didn't know how to answer him, because the truth was, she wasn't sure what she was getting anymore.

Kai shifted beside her, breaking the heavy silence with another laugh. "Come on, Logan, don't scare her off with all your deep questions. We're supposed to be having fun."

Logan's lips twitched in the smallest of smiles, but his eyes remained on Luna for a moment longer before he leaned back in his chair. "Just curious," He said, his tone a little lighter now, though the heat between them hadn't dissipated.

Luna tried to focus on the conversation, but her mind kept drifting to the growing attraction she felt for both men. She couldn't deny it anymore—she was drawn to Logan's quiet intensity just as much as she was to Kai's playful charm. And with each passing moment, the lines between them blurred even more.

Kai, ever the playful instigator, poured more wine into their glasses and leaned in closer to Luna, his arm brushing hers as he grinned. "You know," He said with a wink, "There's a pretty strict rule around here: anyone who gets snowed in has to share a secret."

Luna raised an eyebrow, smiling despite the tension building inside her. "Is that so?"

"Oh, absolutely," Kai said, leaning back and crossing his arms, his grin widening. "And since you're our guest, you get to go first."

Luna glanced between them, her heart racing. She wasn't sure if it was the wine or the situation, but suddenly, the room felt much smaller, the space between her and these two men shrinking with every second. She could feel both their eyes on her, waiting.

"A secret?" She said, trying to buy herself some time. She hadn't expected to be the center of attention like this, and the heat of their gazes made her feel exposed.

Logan's deep voice rumbled softly from his place by the fire. "We won't judge."

Luna laughed nervously, biting her lip as she thought of something to say. The truth was, she had plenty of secrets, but none she was willing to share in this moment. Or maybe it was because of the moment that she wanted to share something real.

"I guess… I've always been afraid of losing control," she said finally, her voice soft. "I'm so used to being in charge at work, in my life. Sometimes, it feels like… I'm not sure what I'm doing anymore."

The confession hung in the air, and for a moment, the playful atmosphere shifted. Luna hadn't expected to reveal something so personal, but there it was, out in the open. She glanced at Kai, expecting another lighthearted comment, but he just smiled at her, softer this time, his blue eyes warm with understanding.

Logan, on the other hand, was watching her with an unreadable expression, his dark eyes filled with something she couldn't quite decipher.

"Control's overrated," Kai said with a wink, breaking the tension. "Sometimes you've just got to let things happen."

Luna smiled at his words, but her heart still raced. Because deep down, she knew that this weekend, trapped in a cabin with these two men, might be the one time in her life where she could let go of control—and the thought terrified and thrilled her in equal measure.

Chapter 5

The storm outside howled with ferocity, the wind rattling the windows as snow piled higher against the cabin walls. Inside, though, the fire blazed brightly, casting a warm glow that contrasted with the biting cold outside. The isolation of the storm, the endless hours spent together, and the undeniable chemistry swirling in the air created an intoxicating atmosphere, one that was impossible to ignore any longer.

It had started innocently enough—a few more glasses of wine after dinner, soft laughter, and shared glances that lingered a moment too long. The small living room had become their haven from the storm, and as the night stretched on, the three of them had settled around the fire, its heat doing little to cool the tension building between them.

Luna sat on the plush rug in front of the fireplace, her legs tucked beneath her as she sipped from her glass. Kai, always the playful one, had sprawled out beside her, leaning back on one elbow with a mischievous smile. Logan, seated in his usual chair, watched them with those dark, smoldering eyes that never failed to send shivers through her.

The wine had loosened them all, the conversation flowing easily, though the undercurrent of desire had grown steadily stronger. Luna could feel it in every shared glance, every accidental brush of skin. It was as if the cabin itself had come alive, trapping them in a bubble of heat and tension.

At some point, the conversation had turned more playful. Kai, always quick with a flirtatious remark, had teased Luna about her fear of skiing, and before she knew it, they were bantering back and forth, their words laced with laughter and innuendo.

"You know," Kai said, his grin widening as he inched closer to her, "I bet you'd be a great skier if you had the right teacher."

Luna laughed, shaking her head. "I doubt even you could make me look graceful on a pair of skis."

Kai's eyes sparkled with amusement, his proximity sending a flutter through her stomach. "You'd be surprised what I can teach."

The teasing should have been light, innocent even, but the way Kai was looking at her now—his blue eyes darkened with something more—made it clear that this was far from innocent. The firelight danced across his face, highlighting the sharp lines of his jaw, and Luna felt her pulse quicken.

And then, as if the moment had been waiting for them all along, Kai leaned in, his lips brushing hers in a soft, playful kiss. It was light at first, tentative, testing the waters. When Luna didn't pull away, when she instead leaned into him, something inside them both ignited.

The kiss deepened, growing bolder as Kai's hand slipped around her waist, pulling her closer. Luna's heart raced, her body reacting to the warmth of his touch, the heat of his mouth on hers. The world outside—the storm, the cold, the blizzard—faded away, leaving only the two of them, caught in the fire of their desire.

Just as the kiss grew more heated, just as Luna's mind began to swirl with the possibilities of where this might lead, she felt a shift. A presence. She pulled back slightly, her breath coming in quick, shallow bursts, and when she opened her eyes, she found Logan standing over them.

He had moved silently, watching them with that same unreadable expression, but now there was something new in his gaze. His eyes were darker than usual, filled with an intensity that made Luna's heart pound even harder. The tension between the three of them reached a breaking point, and for a moment, no one moved.

Then Logan took a step closer.

Luna's pulse raced as she glanced between the two men, caught in the electric charge that filled the air. She had always sensed the pull between her and Logan, even if it had remained unspoken, simmering beneath the surface, but now, standing here, with Kai's arms still wrapped loosely around her waist, the storm outside raging, Logan stepped into the moment as if it had been waiting for him all along.

Without a word, Logan knelt in front of her, his gaze locked on hers. His hand reached out, brushing a strand of hair away from her face, and Luna's breath caught in her throat. The soft touch sent a ripple of anticipation through her, and she felt herself leaning into him, drawn by the magnetic force that had always existed between them.

And then, without hesitation, Logan's lips found hers.

The kiss was nothing like the playful one she had shared with Kai. It was deep, slow, and filled with a smoldering intensity that left no room for doubt. Logan's hand cupped the back of her neck, pulling her closer as his mouth claimed hers with a hunger that matched the storm outside. Luna's mind swirled, her senses overwhelmed by the feel of his lips, his hands, the raw desire that coursed through her.

Kai, still beside her, watched them with an amused smile, but there was something darker in his eyes now, a heat that matched Logan's. When the kiss finally broke, Luna found herself breathless, her heart hammering in her chest as she looked between the two men.

For a moment, everything hung in the balance. Luna's mind raced, trying to process the whirlwind of emotions that had built over the past few days. She had been drawn to both men in different ways, but now, standing at the precipice of something far more complicated and intense, she realized just how deep that attraction went.

Logan's eyes searched hers, his hand still resting on her neck, and Kai's arm tightened around her waist as he leaned in closer, his breath warm against her ear.

"Looks like you don't have to choose," Kai murmured, his voice low and teasing, but laced with the same desire that burned between them all.

Luna shivered, not from the cold, but from the sheer intensity of the moment. The storm outside seemed to grow louder, as if echoing the tempest inside her. She had never been in a situation like this before, caught between two men who both seemed to want her just as much as she wanted them.

Her mind spun with possibilities, her body alive with the tension that pulsed between them. She didn't know what to say, what to do. But as Logan's hand slid down her back and Kai's lips brushed the sensitive skin of her neck, the choice seemed to make itself.

She let go.

The fire roared in the hearth, the storm raged outside, but inside the cabin, everything changed. Luna surrendered to the moment, to the desire that had been building since the moment she stepped through that door. Logan's lips found hers again, claiming her in a kiss that left no room for hesitation, while Kai's hands roamed over her, exploring the curve of her waist, the dip of her spine.

She was caught between them, but there was no fear, no uncertainty—only heat, passion, and the undeniable pull that had drawn them all together in the first place.

The night stretched on, the storm outside raging, but inside, the only storm that mattered was the one they were lost in, together.

Chapter 6

The fire crackled softly in the hearth, its warm glow casting flickering shadows across the cabin's wooden walls. Outside, the storm continued its relentless assault, the wind howling as if in unison with the storm brewing inside the cabin, but the three of them, nestled together on the plush rug in front of the fire, were no longer concerned with the outside world. Time seemed to stretch, each moment heavy with anticipation and the magnetic pull between them.

Luna lay between Logan and Kai, her breath unsteady as her mind tried to keep up with the sudden shift in her reality. She had always thought of herself as someone in control, measured in her decisions, especially when it came to relationships. Now, here in this cabin, with these two impossibly alluring men, she felt like she was freefalling, the ground beneath her crumbling as she surrendered to her desires.

Logan sat beside her, his dark eyes smoldering as they met hers. His touch was slow, deliberate, as his hand slid up her arm, leaving a trail of heat in its wake. There was something about Logan that always left her feeling on edge, his intensity making her pulse race with every glance, every brush of skin. His lips were inches from hers, and the way he looked at her—like he wanted to consume her—set her entire body alight.

On her other side, Kai's presence was just as overwhelming, though in a completely different way. His playfulness, his easy charm, had always made her feel comfortable, but now there was a new kind of tension between them. His fingers trailed over her neck, down to her collarbone, teasing, sending shivers through her body. His lips hovered near her ear, and she felt the warmth of his breath as he whispered, "You're safe here, Luna. Just let go."

She didn't know how to respond—didn't know what to say, how to act. It was as if all of her senses were on overdrive, each touch, each breath, heightening the tension until she felt like she might explode. Her heart pounded in her chest, and she knew, without a doubt, that there was no turning back from this.

The firelight danced in Logan's eyes as he leaned in, his lips brushing hers once more, and this time, there was no hesitation. The kiss was deep, slow, and demanding, filled with the kind of intensity that made her forget everything but him. His hands moved to her waist, pulling her closer, and she felt his body tense against hers, the heat between them growing stronger with every second.

Just as Logan's kiss deepened, Kai's hand slid down her back, his touch possessive and teasing all at once. She gasped against Logan's lips as Kai's fingers traced a slow, deliberate path along her spine, making her arch into Logan's body. The sensation of being between them—torn between their touches, their desires—was dizzying.

Kai's mouth found the sensitive skin of her neck, and Luna couldn't suppress the soft moan that escaped her lips as his tongue teased her, his teeth grazing her skin in a way that sent sparks of pleasure shooting through her. Her hands fisted in Logan's shirt as she was caught in the overwhelming sensations of being claimed by both men at once.

"Luna," Logan murmured against her lips, his voice low and rough, filled with barely restrained desire. "Tell me you want this. Tell us you want this."

Her breath caught in her throat as the weight of the moment settled over her. She did want this—wanted them both, in a way that defied logic or reason. She had never been in a situation like this, but as she lay between Logan and Kai, their touches consuming her, she realized that this was exactly where she was meant to be.

"I want this," she whispered, her voice trembling with a mix of excitement and fear. "I want you both."

Kai's laughter was soft against her skin, his lips brushing the shell of her ear. "Good," he murmured. "Because we're not letting you go."

That was all it took to shatter the fragile barrier that had been holding them back.

Logan's kiss turned more urgent, his hands roaming over her body with a possessiveness that made her head spin. Kai's mouth trailed lower, his lips and hands exploring her skin in ways that left her breathless. The intensity of their touches, the heat of their bodies pressed against hers, was overwhelming, and Luna felt herself spiraling into a whirlwind of desire that she couldn't control.

Time seemed to blur as the three of them became lost in each other, the storm outside mirroring the storm of passion inside. Logan's strength, his quiet intensity, combined with Kai's teasing touches and playful kisses, created a heady mix that left Luna drowning in sensation.

At one point, she found herself in Logan's arms, his lips tracing a path down her neck, while Kai's hands explored her body with a reverence that made her shiver. They moved together as if they had been made for this moment, their touches perfectly synchronized, each knowing exactly when to push and when to pull back.

The fire crackled in the hearth, its warmth wrapping around them as they lost themselves in the night. Logan's kisses grew more demanding, his hands rougher as he pulled her closer, and Luna responded with equal fervor, her body arching into his. Kai's lips followed a trail down her stomach, his touch sending waves of pleasure crashing over her.

The room seemed to spin as the intensity built, their bodies moving together in a rhythm that felt primal, instinctual. Luna had never felt anything like this before—this all-consuming desire, this need to be with them both, to let them take her, claim her.

Logan's grip tightened on her waist as he whispered against her lips, "You belong to us tonight."

And Luna, lost in the haze of pleasure and need, knew that it was true. For this night, for this moment, she belonged to them—completely.

As the night wore on, the storm outside reached its peak, the wind and snow battering the cabin. But inside, the fire between them burned brighter, hotter, until there was nothing left but the heat of their bodies entwined, the sound of their shared breaths, and the undeniable connection that had drawn them together.

Chapter 7

The cabin was warm and inviting, the scent of wood smoke and rain soaked air, mixed with the musky smell of their bodies, enveloped her as she lay there between them. She could feel the heat of their skin against hers, their heartbeats pounding in sync. Logan's chest rose and fell against her back as he took a deep breath, his strong, broad shoulders moving with his every exhale. She looked down at Kai, his dark eyes locked onto hers, the desire in them burning brightly. He leaned in, his lips brushing against hers lightly, teasingly, before he pulled away, his hand trailing down her stomach, teasing the skin of her lower abdomen.

"You're so beautiful, Luna," He whispered, his voice low and gravelly. "So soft and responsive."

She moaned softly, arching into his touch, her body craving more. His fingers continued to dance over her skin, exploring and prodding, finding her sensitive spots. Then his warm hand slid into her pants and past the waistband of her panties. She held her breath as he found her core, his touch sending shivers of pleasure through her. He slid a finger inside her, his eyes locked on hers, and she gasped, feeling the heat between her legs intensify as he started to rub gently.

"Oh, god," she cried out softly, her body starting to shake with pleasure. His touch was electrifying, sending a bolt of pleasure racing through her, straight to her core. She arched into his hand, moaning loudly.

Logan watched them intently, his chest heaving as he tried to control himself. He leaned forward, kissing her neck, his lips trailing hotly down her collarbone. She could feel his erection pressing against her backside and it made her shiver. Luna's eyes fluttered open, her heart racing as a wave of desire coursed through her. The storm outside the cabin had quieted down, the wind dying away and the snowfall slowing to a gentle patter against the roof. Inside, the fire crackled and popped, casting flickering shadows on the logs of the cabin. Logan and Kai were still there, their bodies intertwined with hers, their breathing heavy and ragged.

Kai's finger slid in and out of her slowly, his touch sending shivers down her spine. She could feel the heat between her legs intensify as he played with her, his other hand cupping her breast, teasing the tip of her nipple. Luna closed her eyes, luxuriating in the sensation, her body arching into his touch. She felt Logan's warm breath against the side of her neck, his hand moving up and down her stomach in soft, gentle strokes.

"Open your eyes, love," Kai whispered.

She obeyed, her gaze locking with his. He smiled, his blunt teeth glistening in the firelight as he pushed another finger inside her. Luna gasped, her back arching off the floor in response to the intense sensation. Logan's mouth found her ear, his lips brushing against her skin, sending shivers down her spine.

"You're so wet for us," He whispered, his voice hoarse. "You're so fucking sexy."

Luna couldn't tear her eyes away from Kai's as he continued to finger her, his other hand trailing up her thigh, stopping at the junction of her legs. She squirmed, wanting more, needing him to touch her there. Kai smiled, his eyes dark with need.

Kai moved his fingers deeper inside her, his lips finding hers in a soft, teasing kiss. Luna moaned into his mouth, her body writhing under his touch. She felt Logan's hands move to her hips, gripping her tightly, pulling her back into his body. The heat from both men filled her senses, overwhelming her with their combined strength and passion.

As Kai's fingers moved in and out of her, she could feel the roughness of his fingertips against her sensitive skin, sending shivers of pleasure down her spine. She gasped, arching her back, as he added a third finger, hitting a spot deep inside her that made her whole body tremble. His other hand moved up her leg, pressing against her swollen clit, rubbing soft circles that sent sparks of pleasure coursing through her.

Luna's eyes drifted shut, focusing on the sensations Kai was creating within her. The warmth of the cabin faded away, replaced by the heat of their bodies and the friction of their skin on skin. She could feel Logan's lips on her neck, his hot breath sending shivers down her back. His hands roamed over her hips, grabbing hold of her ass.

Their kisses grew deeper, more intense, as Kai continued to play with her, his fingers moving faster, his breath hot against her ear. Luna moaned loudly, her body quivering under their touch. She could feel the tension building inside her, the need growing stronger with each passing moment. Kai's fingers picked up speed, his hand pressing firmly against her clit, and she cried out, her hips bucking off the floor.

Luna's eyes snapped open as she felt the rush of pleasure, her vision blurring. Stars exploded behind her eyelids as Kai's fingers danced inside her, his lips marking her skin with hot, open-mouthed kisses. Logan's grip on her hips tightened, pulling her harder against him, and she felt him swell against her, pressing against her ass. She moaned loudly as Kai's fingers found her G-spot, his touch driving her wild with desire. She whimpered, arching into his hand, wanting more.

The cabin was alive with their moans and gasps, every inch of skin touching skin on skin raising the temperature. The scent of their arousal filled the air, mingling with the smoky scent from the fireplace. Logan's other hand joined Kai's, both of them rubbing her clit in sync, sending shockwaves of pleasure coursing through her body.

Her eyes snapped shut, her muscles tensed and her core clenched around Kai's fingers as the orgasm overtook her, waves of pleasure crashing over her. Luna cried out, her body shaking as she came undone, Kai's fingers thrusting deeper into her as she writhed under their touch.

As she lay on her back, trying to catch her breath she felt Kai and Logan move. Then the sound of fabric rustling and what made her eye open was the sound of metal clinking.

They were undressing.

As she watched them shed their clothes her stomach fluttered. These men were gorgeous.

Logan and Kai moved towards her, their hard cocks rubbing against each other as they positioned themselves on the sides of her body. They leaned in to kiss her neck, their hot breath sending shivers down her spine. Their hands trailed down her body, caressing and squeezing every inch of her skin.

Kai's tongue traced a line from her earlobe to her jawline, his stubble scratching softly against her skin. He nipped at her bottom lip, pulling away with a teasing smile when she tried to deepen the kiss. "Look at us," he whispered hoarsely, nodding his head towards where they stood naked before her.

Luna gasped at the sight of their bodies on full display: Logan's muscles rippling beneath tanned skin, his six-pack leading up to a thick chest covered in dark hair; Kai's lean frame accentuated by the veins snaking across his abdomen and thighs. Their cocks stood proudly before her, twitching in anticipation.

"You're so beautiful," Logan murmured, capturing one of her breasts in his hand. He rolled the hardened nipple between his fingers as he leaned in to suckle on it hungrily. Luna arched into his touch, moaning softly as he flicked his tongue over it while Kai took hold of her other breast and did the same.

Luna felt something ignite in her, reached below, and slid her pants off, kicking them to the side. "Please, I want it," she begged, she could feel her own slick dripping out of her. Logan and Kai looked at each other as if talking telepathically. Then after what felt like forever, Logan shifted. He slid in between her thighs, positioning the head of his cock at her entrance.

With a rough, possessive groan, Logan pushed forward, filling her up in one swift thrust. Luna's eyes shot open as she felt the thick head of his cock breach her tight walls. His hips slammed into hers, burying him deep inside her. She gasped and arching her back as the intense fullness overwhelmed her. Kai watched them intensely from above, his cock leaking pre-cum onto her stomach.

Logan began to move slowly, drawing out each thrust as he pulled almost completely out before pushing back in again. His muscles flexed under his tan skin with every pull of his hips, highlighting the rippling strength of his body. He growled low in his throat with each push, hitting her G-spot perfectly with every stroke. His hand found its way to her clit, rubbing it roughly between thrusts while he kissed down her neck and collarbone.

As Logan pounded into her, there was a cacophony of wet smacks and slaps as their skin met, a symphony of lustful pleasure that seemed to fill the entire cabin.

Her eyes rolled back in her head as he slowly thrusted in and out, each motion bringing pleasure unlike any she had felt before. The friction was incredible, making her moan and buck her hips up to meet him deeper.

Kai watched hungrily from above, his cock now heavy and throbbing in anticipation.

The smell of sweat and sex filled the air, mingling with the scent of their arousal as they moved together in unison. Their skin glistened with perspiration as they picked up speed, their moans echoing off the wooden walls around them. Luna could feel that winding pressure growing inside her. She was coming and coming fast.

She opened her mouth in a silent scream as they brought her over the edge again, moaning into his skin as her inner walls clenched and pulsed around Logan's cock. Her nails bit into his shoulders, drawing thin lines of blood that only fueled their lust more. Logan pulled out suddenly, leaving her empty and needy before slamming back in with a loud smack that echoed through the room.

"Fuck!" Logan shouted as he poured himself inside her. After he stilled for a few seconds he pulled himself out of her sopping cunt. Before Luna could process it, she was being turned over on her stomach. Kai was on her like an animal, his face unreadable as he positioned himself at her wet entrance.

There was a moment of hesitation before he plunged in, filling her up once more.

She let out a moan of pleasure that echoed through the cabin.

Kai's thrusts were different from Logan's; they were shorter and harder, each one sending shockwaves of pleasure through her core. His hands found her hips, holding her in place as he began fucking her at a relentless pace. She could feel his chest hair tickling her back, his muscles flexing with every powerful stroke.

The sounds of skin slapping skin filled the air as they moved together, their breathing heavy and ragged. The smell of sex and sweat was almost overwhelming now, mixed with the cool wood smoke from the fireplace. The heat from their bodies made the room almost stifling, but they didn't care. She could feel herself getting close again.

Kai growled low in his throat and held onto her hips tighter, slamming into her harder as he felt her walls tightening around him.

"I'm coming!" Luna shouted. "It's too much!"

Kai growled in response, pushing harder into her. "Take it all," he grunted as he felt her walls clenching around him. He slapped his thick cock against her ass cheeks, the slap echoing in the small room. Logan grabbed onto her hips, his grip tight as he watched on from behind, his own cock twitching as he got closer to cumming

With a loud groan, he buried himself inside her once more, filling her up completely. It was more than enough for Luna, who was drowning in pleasure at this point. Her eyes rolled back once again.

Luna's body shook violently as another powerful orgasm ripped through her. Her vision went white as waves of intense pleasure crashed over her again and again. She cried out Kai's name, her voice hoarse and desperate as he continued pounding into her.

Kai's thrusts became erratic as he neared his own climax. With a primal roar, he slammed into her one final time, spilling himself deep inside her. His cock pulsed as he emptied every last drop, their mixed fluids dripping down Luna's thighs.

Panting heavily, Kai slowly pulled out and collapsed beside her.

Luna lay there trembling, completely spent and overwhelmed by the intensity of what had just happened. Logan moved to her other side, running his hand soothingly along her back.

For several long moments, the only sounds in the cabin were their heavy breathing. As they lay there catching their breath, the crackling of the fire filled the silence. Luna's body tingled all over, waves of aftershocks still pulsing through her core. She felt utterly satisfied yet somehow still hungry for more.

Logan was the first to move, propping himself up on one elbow to gaze down at Luna. His eyes roamed over her flushed skin, a look of awe and desire on his face. He reached out to brush a strand of hair from her forehead, his touch impossibly gentle after the intensity of their lovemaking.

"You're incredible," He murmured, leaning in to place a soft kiss on her lips.

On her other side, Kai stirred, rolling onto his side to face them. His hand found Luna's hip, thumb tracing lazy circles on her skin. "That was…" He trailed off, shaking his head in amazement.

Luna smiled, basking in the warmth of their bodies pressed against her. She felt deliciously sore and thoroughly satisfied. "That was incredible," she agreed, her voice still husky.

Logan's hand trailed down her side, igniting sparks across her sensitive skin. "We're not done with you yet," he growled softly in her ear.

A shiver of anticipation ran through her. Despite her exhaustion, she felt a fresh wave of arousal pooling between her thighs.

Kai's hand slid lower, fingers ghosting over her inner thigh. "Think you can handle another round?" he asked, a wicked glint in his eye. Luna bit her lip, considering. Her body was tired, but the desire building inside her was impossible to ignore.

She nodded slowly. "I want more," she whispered.

Chapter 8

The soft glow of early morning light filtered through the curtains, casting a pale golden hue across the cabin. Luna stirred beneath the blankets, her body heavy with warmth and the lingering aftershocks of the night before. As she blinked awake, the first thing she noticed was the steady rise and fall of two chests beside her.

Kai was on her left, his arm draped possessively over her waist, his blond hair tousled from sleep, a peaceful expression softening his sharp features. On her right, Logan lay close, his muscular arm still around her, his face buried in the pillow. Even in sleep, his presence radiated a quiet intensity that made her pulse quicken.

For a moment, Luna stayed completely still, her mind slowly catching up to the reality of her situation. She was in bed with both of them. Logan and Kai. The events of the night before flooded back in vivid detail—whispered promises, heated kisses, and the way their bodies had moved together like they had been waiting for that moment for longer than she could have imagined.

The blizzard had been a catalyst, trapping them in a world where time and rules no longer seemed to apply. And now, with the storm finally over, the sunlight streaming into the cabin felt like a reminder that life was about to intrude once more.

For now, she was wrapped in the warmth of two men who had, for one night, made her feel alive in a way she had never known before.

Luna shifted slightly, trying not to disturb them as she adjusted her position. The sheets rustled softly, and she felt Kai stir beside her, his eyes fluttering open. When he saw her watching him, a slow, lazy smile spread across his face.

"Good morning," He whispered, his voice thick with sleep. He reached out to brush a strand of hair away from her face, his touch gentle but filled with affection.

"Morning," she replied softly, her heart fluttering at the intimacy of the moment.

Kai leaned in, pressing a soft kiss to her forehead, and for a brief second, everything felt normal, as if waking up sandwiched between two men was just part of her life, but then her gaze drifted to Logan, still asleep beside her, and the weight of the situation hit her all over again. How had this happened? What did it mean for all of them?

As if sensing her thoughts, Kai's smile faltered slightly. "You okay?" He asked, his tone light but laced with concern.

Luna hesitated, unsure of how to answer. She didn't want to break the fragile peace that hung between them, but the questions swirling in her mind were impossible to ignore. She wasn't sure how to navigate this new reality—this attraction to two men, this connection that felt far more intense than she had ever expected.

"I'm… I'm not sure," she admitted quietly, her voice barely above a whisper.

"It's a lot to process."

Kai's eyes softened, and he nodded in understanding. "Yeah, it is," He said, his thumb brushing lightly over her wrist. "...But we'll figure it out. No rush."

Before Luna could respond, Logan stirred beside her, his brow furrowing slightly as he woke. His dark eyes opened slowly, and for a moment, he seemed disoriented, blinking against the light. When he saw Luna lying between him and Kai, a flicker of something intense crossed his features. His hand, still resting on her waist, tightened slightly, and his gaze held hers in a way that made her breath catch.

"Morning," He said, his voice rough from sleep, but there was no mistaking the lingering heat in his tone.

"Morning," Luna replied, her voice softer than she intended. The intensity of Logan's gaze made her heart race, and she felt the familiar tension building between them all over again, despite the early hour.

Logan's eyes flicked to Kai, then back to her, and the three of them seemed to hold the moment in suspension. There was no denying what had happened the night before, and now, in the clear light of day, the weight of that reality hung heavily between them. Instead of awkwardness, there was something else in the air—something charged, but unspoken.

It was Kai who finally broke the silence, his tone light and teasing as he stretched beside them. "Well, this is one hell of a way to wake up."

Luna laughed softly, some of the tension easing as she let herself relax into the moment. She couldn't deny that waking up between them was... exhilarating, even if her mind was a whirlwind of confusion and questions. There was something comforting about the way they both seemed so at ease, as if they had been expecting this all along.

Then, as the reality of the morning settled in, so did the questions that had been lurking in the back of Luna's mind. What happened next? Was this just a one-time thing, a fleeting moment of passion born out of isolation and desire? Or was there something deeper at play?

She felt Logan shift beside her, his hand sliding gently from her waist to her back, a possessive gesture that made her stomach flip. His eyes, dark and thoughtful, studied her face for a long moment before he spoke.

"Are you okay with this?" He asked, his voice quiet but firm, as if he needed to know, needed her to say the words out loud.

Luna swallowed, her throat tight. Was she okay with this? With them? The truth was, she didn't know. What she did know was that last night had felt right, more right than anything had in a long time. Being with them, feeling their touches, their affection—it had unlocked something inside her that she hadn't even realized she was missing.

"I… I think I am," she whispered, her voice shaky but honest. "I just don't know what this means."

Kai shifted, propping himself up on one elbow, his eyes soft but serious now. "It doesn't have to mean anything right now," He said gently. "We're snowed in, no rush to figure anything out. Let's just… take things as they come."

Logan nodded, his fingers trailing up and down her back in slow, soothing strokes. "No pressure, Luna," He murmured. "We're here with you, whatever happens."

His words were a comfort, but they didn't entirely quiet the storm inside her. She was drawn to them both in ways that defied logic or explanation. And as she lay there, surrounded by their warmth, she realized that for the first time in her life, she wasn't in control—and maybe that was okay.

For now, the storm outside had passed, but inside the cabin, something new had begun to brew. Something unpredictable, something that both excited and terrified her.

Luna closed her eyes, allowing herself to be fully present in this moment. She could feel the heat of Kai's body against hers, the steady thrum of Logan's pulse beneath her fingers. It was overwhelming, but she wasn't alone in this. Whatever was to come, they would face it together—at least for now.

And in the stillness of the morning, with the remnants of the storm swirling outside, she allowed herself to let go of her fears, if only for a little while.

Chapter 9

❧

The storm had left the mountain buried in snow, cutting them off from the outside world for days. As time passed, the isolation of the cabin shifted from feeling like a temporary refuge to an intimate sanctuary, where the lines between Luna, Logan, and Kai blurred further with each passing hour. What had begun as a spark of passion between them had turned into a fire, each day—and each night—bringing new and more intense encounters.

Luna had never experienced anything like it before, the pull she felt toward both men. The contrast between them was thrilling, a constant push and pull that kept her off balance. And as they remained snowed in, their connection deepened, both emotionally and physically.

Kai was the light in the darkness, his playful nature making her feel at ease even in the most intense moments. His kisses were teasing at first, full of laughter and sweetness, but as their nights together stretched longer, that teasing gave way to something more—something raw and passionate. There was a fire inside him, one that she hadn't fully seen until she found herself in his arms, lost in the way his lips could leave her breathless and wanting more.

On those steamy nights, Kai's touch was electric. His body moved against hers with a confidence that left her dizzy, each kiss, each caress growing more urgent, more demanding. He had a way of making her feel like the only person in the world, his whispers in her ear both playful and intense, driving her to the edge until she could barely think.

One night, after a dinner filled with laughter and wine, they ended up on the rug in front of the fire again, just as they had on that first night. Kai's laughter faded into soft gasps as their kisses deepened, his hands exploring her with a tenderness that soon gave way to something more primal. The heat between them was overwhelming, and Luna felt herself surrendering to the moment, her body trembling beneath his touch.

"Kai," she breathed, her fingers clutching at his back as his lips traced a path down her neck. His name fell from her lips like a plea, and he responded with a low growl of satisfaction, his hands gripping her waist as he pulled her closer.

He pressed her into the soft rug, his body covering hers, the warmth of the fire surrounding them. "I've got you, Luna," he murmured, his voice rough with desire. "I'm not letting go."

And in that moment, with the crackling fire and Kai's weight pressing down on her, Luna let herself be consumed by him. There was something about the way he touched her—like he was claiming her, piece by piece—that left her breathless. His passion was infectious, and she couldn't help but lose herself in it, the nights spent with him filled with an intensity that left her wanting more.

While Kai was all heat and fire, Logan was something entirely different—something darker, something that simmered beneath the surface and threatened to erupt at any moment.

Logan's desire for her was a slow burn, his every touch deliberate, calculated.

His intense gaze often left her feeling exposed, as if he could see straight through her. During the day, there were moments when their connection felt almost volatile—heated exchanges that had nothing to do with words but everything to do with the energy crackling between them. And at night, that slow-burning desire flared into something far more dangerous.

One evening, after a particularly tense day spent clearing snow from the cabin's entryway, Luna had found herself alone in the kitchen with Logan. The air between them had been charged since the moment she'd stepped in, his silence somehow more potent than anything he could have said. As she turned to grab something from the counter, she felt him behind her, the space between them practically vibrating with tension.

"Logan," she started, but before she could say more, he had her backed up against the counter, his hands on either side of her, trapping her in. His eyes were dark, smoldering, filled with an intensity that stole the breath from her lungs.

"Luna," He said quietly, his voice rough and low, "you drive me insane."

Her heart hammered in her chest as she stared up at him, her pulse quickening at the raw emotion in his eyes. She could feel his body pressing against hers, the heat radiating off him like a furnace. And then, just as her mind began to whirl with thoughts of what was about to happen, Logan's lips crashed down on hers.

The kiss was fierce, a collision of need and frustration that left her reeling. His hands gripped her hips, pulling her against him as his mouth moved hungrily over hers. There was nothing soft or playful about Logan's kisses—they were demanding, full of intensity and fire that set her blood racing. His desire for her had always simmered beneath the surface, but now, with his hands roaming her body, it had exploded into something all-consuming.

Their nights together were charged with the same energy, each encounter a battle of wills, a constant push and pull. Logan wasn't gentle like Kai—he was possessive, dominant, his touches filled with a hunger that left no room for hesitation. And Luna responded in kind, meeting his intensity with her own, their physical connection growing more heated with each passing day.

One night, after one of their more heated arguments—over something insignificant that neither of them could even remember afterward—they had ended up tangled in the sheets, their bodies pressed together as if the confrontation had only served to stoke the fire between them. Logan's lips had found hers in the darkness, his hands gripping her wrists as he pinned her to the bed, his breath hot against her ear.

"You drive me crazy," He growled, his voice thick with desire. "I can't stop thinking about you."

Luna's breath had caught in her throat as she felt his body press against hers, the weight of him overwhelming her senses. She had never experienced anything like it—the sheer force of his desire for her, the way he seemed to lose control every time they were together.

Their encounters were raw, primal, and filled with an intensity that left her shaken. Logan's passion was a slow burn, but when it ignited, it consumed everything in its path.

As the days passed, Luna found herself caught between them—between Kai's playful, consuming passion and Logan's slow, deliberate desire. Each encounter with them left her more conflicted, the lines between affection, lust, and love blurring until she wasn't sure where one ended and the other began.

But even as her body surrendered to them, her mind couldn't help but wonder: how long could this last? How could she possibly choose between them, when each of them gave her something the other couldn't?

And as the snow outside began to thaw, signaling the end of their time in isolation, Luna knew the answer was growing more elusive with each passing day. The storm might have brought them together, but what would happen when reality came crashing back in?

Would their connection survive once the outside world returned? Or would it fade, like the melting snow, leaving her with nothing but memories of the passion they had shared in the quiet of the cabin?

As she lay in bed one night, between Kai's warm, comforting embrace and Logan's possessive hold, Luna knew the time to face the truth was coming. For now, she let herself fall deeper into the storm they had created, unwilling to let go of the intensity that had changed everything.

Chapter 10

The snow had stopped falling, and the sun broke through the clouds for the first time in days, casting a blinding light over the once-impassable roads. The world outside the cabin looked fresh and untouched, a perfect blanket of white stretching across the mountains. The storm had finally cleared, leaving behind a crisp, quiet stillness that seemed to contrast sharply with the turmoil inside Luna's heart.

Luna stood by the window, watching as the sunlight reflected off the snow, her packed bags resting by the door. The time had come to leave the cabin, to return to the world she had left behind, but everything inside her felt tangled in knots. Her time with Logan and Kai had been intense, transformative even, and now that the moment of truth had arrived, she felt more conflicted than ever.

Both men had given her something she hadn't even realized she was missing—Kai with his lighthearted warmth and playful passion, Logan with his slow-burning intensity and fierce need for her. They had both drawn her in, made her feel alive in a way she hadn't felt in years, and now she was faced with a choice she wasn't sure she could make.

The sound of footsteps behind her broke through her thoughts, and she turned to see Kai approaching, his easy smile still present, but his blue eyes clouded with something more serious. He stopped beside her, his hands slipping into his pockets as he glanced out the window.

"Beautiful, isn't it?" he said, his voice quiet.

Luna nodded, her heart heavy in her chest. "Yeah," she whispered. "It is."

Kai leaned against the windowsill, his gaze flicking back to her. "So… you're really leaving today."

It wasn't a question, but a statement, and Luna felt the weight of it settle over her. She swallowed hard, unable to meet his eyes for a moment. "I think I have to."

Kai nodded slowly, his smile fading as he studied her face. "I get it. This whole thing… it's been unexpected, to say the least…But I don't regret a second of it, Luna. Not one."

His words sent a wave of emotion crashing through her, and she bit her lip to keep it from trembling. Kai had a way of making everything feel light, even when the situation was heavy. His playful, carefree nature had drawn her in from the beginning, but there was a depth to him too—one she had only fully realized over the past few days. He wasn't just a flirt or a tease. He cared deeply, and that scared her because it made her care too.

"I don't regret it either, Kai," she said softly. "You've… you've made this whole experience unforgettable."

Kai's smile returned, though it didn't quite reach his eyes this time. He reached out, gently brushing a strand of hair behind her ear, his touch tender. "Whatever you decide, I just want you to know, I'm here. If you need me."

Luna's throat tightened as she nodded, her chest aching with the weight of the unspoken words between them. Kai had been the light in the darkness, the laughter that had kept her grounded, but as much as she cared for him, there was another part of her that was equally drawn to the man standing across the room, watching them in silence.

Logan.

He leaned against the doorframe, arms crossed, his expression unreadable but his dark eyes locked on hers. There was something in his gaze, something intense and raw, that made her pulse quicken. Logan had always been the more serious of the two, the one who held back his emotions until they burned too hot to control. And now, standing there, he looked like he was barely holding back the storm inside him.

Kai noticed the shift in the air and gave a small nod. "I'll give you two a moment," He said quietly, stepping back and heading toward the kitchen, leaving Luna and Logan alone in the cabin.

For a long moment, neither of them spoke. The tension between them, always simmering, was now nearly unbearable. Finally, Logan pushed away from the doorframe, moving toward her with slow, deliberate steps. His gaze never left hers, and when he stopped in front of her, Luna felt her breath catch in her throat.

"You're leaving," Logan said, his voice low and rough, as if the words themselves were painful to say.

Luna nodded, her chest tight. "I have to."

Logan's jaw tightened, and he reached out, cupping her face in his hands, his touch both firm and gentle. His dark eyes searched hers, and she saw the vulnerability there—the fear of losing her, the desperation to hold on to whatever they had found together.

"I don't want you to go," He murmured, his voice hoarse. "...But I know I can't ask you to stay."

Luna's heart clenched at the raw honesty in his words. Logan had never been one to speak his emotions easily, but when he did, it was with a depth that shook her to her core. She had felt it in every kiss, every touch—the way he wanted her, needed her—but also the way he respected her, enough to let her make her own choice.

"I don't know what to do, Logan," she admitted, her voice trembling. "I'm so torn. This... these past few days... they've changed everything."

Logan's thumb brushed lightly over her cheek, his gaze never leaving hers. "Then don't make any decisions right now," He said softly. "Go, take the time you need, but know this—you're not just running from one life into another. You'll have to decide what you really want."

Luna closed her eyes, leaning into his touch for a brief moment, savoring the warmth and the safety she felt in his arms. The idea of leaving him—leaving both of them—felt impossible, but staying meant facing something she wasn't sure she was ready for.

When she finally opened her eyes, Logan was watching her with the same intensity as always, but this time there was a softness too, an acceptance of whatever decision she would make.

"I care about you, Luna," Logan said quietly. "More than I ever expected to...But I need you to be sure. I need you to know that whatever happens next, it's your choice."

The weight of his words pressed down on her, and she realized in that moment that Logan wasn't asking her to choose between him and Kai—not yet. He was asking her to choose what kind of life she wanted, who she wanted to be moving forward.

And that was the hardest decision of all.

With her heart heavy, Luna reached up and kissed Logan softly, pouring every ounce of emotion she had into that kiss. When they pulled apart, she whispered, "I don't know what the future holds, but I'll never forget this."

Logan's eyes darkened, and he nodded, his hand still resting on her cheek. "Neither will I."

The sound of a car engine broke the silence, and Luna turned to see that the snowplows had finally cleared the roads. It was time to go.

With a deep breath, she picked up her bags and headed for the door, her mind spinning with everything that had happened. As she stepped outside, the cold mountain air hit her, a sharp reminder of the reality waiting beyond the cabin's walls.

Kai was standing by the door, his eyes shadowed but filled with the same warmth she had come to know so well. He didn't say anything, just gave her a soft smile that told her everything she needed to know. He would always be there if she needed him.

And with one last glance at the cabin, at the two men who had changed her life in ways she never could have imagined, Luna walked out into the snow, knowing that the decision she had to make would shape everything from here on out.

She just didn't know what that decision would be—yet.

Chapter 11

The car engine hummed softly beneath Luna as she drove down the winding mountain road, the towering snow-capped peaks slowly shrinking in her rearview mirror. After what felt like an hour Luna had managed to dig out her car just enough. The sun glinted off the white blanket covering the landscape, and while the storm had cleared, Luna's thoughts were anything but settled.

The days spent in the cabin with Logan and Kai had been more than just a whirlwind of passion—they had shifted something inside her, forcing her to confront feelings and desires she hadn't even known she had. But what had started as an escape from the pressures of her life had become a deeper, more complex connection than she could have anticipated.

As the miles passed, Luna's decision crystallized. She had come to the mountains seeking clarity and escape, but what she had found was something far more profound—a love that didn't fit neatly into any box, and an undeniable connection with two men who, in their own ways, had shown her pieces of herself she hadn't known were missing.

A part of her had wanted to run, to leave and pretend that the feelings swirling inside her would fade with distance. But another part—the part that was tired of pretending to be someone she wasn't—knew she couldn't walk away from what had happened in that cabin. Not when it had awakened something so raw, so real.

It had been a week since she left the cabin, and the pull to return had only grown stronger. Luna had taken time for herself, reflecting on what she wanted—not just from love, but from life. The memories of her time with Logan and Kai lingered in her thoughts, not just the physical connection, but the emotional bond that had developed between the three of them. They had each given her something different, something she couldn't deny she needed.

Now, she stood outside the cabin once more, the same cabin where everything had changed. This time, the roads were clear, the sky bright and blue, and yet her heart pounded in her chest just as fiercely as it had the day the storm had first thrown her into their lives.

With a deep breath, Luna knocked on the door.

It swung open, and Kai's familiar grin greeted her. His expression shifted from surprise to warmth in an instant, and he stepped forward, pulling her into a hug. "Luna," He said, his voice filled with genuine happiness. "You came back."

She smiled against his chest, her heart fluttering at the simple warmth of being in his arms again. Logan who was sitting in a chair stood up, placing down a book he was reading. "I had to," she whispered. "What….what we had in the cabin… it wasn't just about one of you. It was about all three of us. And I don't want to walk away from that."

Logan's eyes darkened with understanding, and Kai's smile faltered for a moment before a new light sparked in his eyes.

Luna took a deep breath, gathering her courage. "I don't know if this is crazy, or if it can even work, but I don't want to lose either of you. I care about both of you, and I don't want to pretend that what we shared wasn't real. I think… I think there's a way for us to make this work. Together."

The words hung in the air, and for a moment, everything was still. Luna's heart raced as she watched their reactions, her pulse pounding in her ears. She had no idea how they would respond, no idea if they would even want the same thing. But she had to be honest, had to take the leap, because walking away from both of them felt impossible.

Kai was the first to speak, his grin slowly returning, though this time there was something more serious behind it. "You really think we can do this, Luna?" He asked, his voice filled with warmth and a touch of awe. "Because I've never stopped wanting you. I've been thinking about you every day since you left."

Logan remained silent, his gaze locked on hers. His expression was unreadable, and for a moment, Luna's heart sank. But then, after what felt like an eternity, Logan stepped forward, his hand gently cupping her face.

"We can make this work," he said quietly, his voice rough with emotion. "But only if we're all in this together. No half measures, no games."

Luna nodded, her chest tightening with relief. "I'm in," she whispered. "All the way."

Kai let out a breath of relief, a laugh escaping him as he pulled both Logan and Luna into his arms. "Well then," he said with a grin, "looks like we're rewriting the rules."

The weeks that followed were a whirlwind of adjustment, passion, and discovery. Navigating an unconventional relationship wasn't easy—it came with challenges, moments of uncertainty, and conversations they had never imagined having. But it also came with joy, with laughter, and with the kind of connection Luna had never thought possible.

They found a rhythm that worked for them, learning how to share each other's time, affection, and love in a way that felt natural. Luna would spend her mornings with Logan, sharing quiet moments over coffee, their conversations deep and thoughtful, their physical connection slow and simmering. The intensity between them never faded, and Logan's need for her remained a constant fire that kept her on edge in the best possible way.

In the afternoons, Kai's playful energy filled the cabin. They would cook together, laughing over spilled ingredients and shared kisses, their time together always light, but no less passionate. Kai's touch was always teasing, always exploring, and his ability to make her feel like the center of his world left Luna breathless every time they were together.

And at night, the three of them would come together, their connection growing stronger with each passing day. The intimacy they shared was unlike anything Luna had ever experienced—unconventional, yes, but fulfilling in ways she hadn't thought possible. The nights were filled with laughter, with whispered confessions, and with the kind of passion that only deepened as their bond grew.

There were challenges, of course. Navigating jealousy, insecurities, and the practicalities of balancing a relationship between three people required patience and communication. But they were committed to making it work, to being honest with one another, and to rewriting the rules of what love could look like.

For the first time in her life, Luna felt truly free—free to love both Logan and

Kai without reservation, free to live her life on her own terms, and free to explore a new kind of relationship that defied expectations. The connection she shared with both men was real, and it was enough. Together, they had created something beautiful, something that worked for them, even if the rest of the world didn't understand.

And as the three of them lay together one evening, the fire crackling softly in the background, Luna smiled, knowing that she had found a new kind of love—one that didn't fit into a neat little box, but one that was hers, and theirs, to hold on to.

For as long as they chose to.

Epilogue

The crisp mountain air stung Luna's cheeks as she stood at the top of the beginner ski slope, looking out over the stunning white expanse below. The snow glittered under the bright midday sun, stretching endlessly across the mountainside. It was the perfect winter day—the kind that beckoned adventurers to the slopes and left the whole world shimmering in icy brilliance.

But as Luna peered down the gentle incline of the bunny slope, she couldn't help the nervous flutter in her stomach.

Behind her, Kai appeared with his usual carefree grin, gliding effortlessly on his skis and stopping gracefully beside her. He leaned on his poles and gave her a teasing wink.

"Don't worry, Luna," he said, laughter in his voice. "I won't let you fall too many times. But I'm not making any promises."

Luna rolled her eyes, but a smile tugged at her lips. Kai's lightheartedness was infectious, and even though the idea of skiing still filled her with trepidation, his presence always managed to calm her nerves.

On her other side, Logan appeared, his usual serious expression softened by the warmth in his dark eyes. He moved with precision, his skis carving clean lines in the snow as he joined them. Unlike Kai's teasing, Logan's approach was more grounded, a steadying force that kept her from letting her anxiety take over.

"You've got this," Logan said, his voice low and reassuring as he adjusted the strap of her ski poles. "Just keep your knees bent, take it slow, and trust yourself. We're right here with you."

Luna took a deep breath and nodded. She appreciated the balance between them—Kai's playfulness and Logan's calm presence, just as she had throughout their time together. It was what made their unconventional relationship work, and now, standing here on the slopes with both of them, she felt a sense of completeness.

Today was the start of something new for her, not just with Logan and Kai, but within herself. The past few months had been filled with growth, discovery, and moments that challenged everything she thought she knew about love, life, and relationships. She had learned to trust herself, to embrace the things that made her heart race, and now she was doing the same on the slopes.

The three of them had spent weeks planning this day—a lighthearted ski lesson that was meant to be both a celebration of their shared time in the mountains and a small victory for Luna, who had always been nervous about skiing. And though the relationship they shared was far from conventional, it was the one thing in her life that made perfect sense.

"Ready to fall on your butt?" Kai teased, nudging her playfully with his elbow.

Luna grinned, her nerves loosening slightly. "Not if I can help it," she shot back.

Kai laughed and motioned toward the slope. "Alright, here's what we'll do. You'll start at the top, we'll guide you, and when you're ready, you'll let gravity do the rest. Trust me, you'll be flying down this thing in no time."

Logan stepped in, his hand resting lightly on her lower back, a grounding touch. "Start slow. If you need to stop, angle your skis. Remember, you're in control. Just follow my lead."

With both men at her side, Luna felt a surge of confidence. They had been through so much together, and if she could navigate the complexities of their relationship, she could definitely handle a simple bunny slope.

Taking a deep breath, she positioned herself at the top of the slope, her skis pointed straight ahead. Kai gave her a wink, and Logan offered a small nod of encouragement. Then, without thinking too much about it, she pushed off.

The first few feet were shaky. Her skis wobbled, her knees locked, and for a brief second, she felt panic rising in her chest. But then she heard Kai's laughter behind her, light and carefree, and Logan's steady voice guiding her, reminding her to bend her knees and trust herself.

As she gained speed, Luna's nerves faded, replaced by the exhilaration of gliding over the snow. The wind rushed past her face, and her body began to move naturally with the rhythm of the slope. It wasn't perfect—she could hear Kai and Logan shouting instructions and encouragement from behind—but for the first time, she felt in control.

"Keep going! You're doing great!" Kai called, his voice full of pride.

"Nice and easy," Logan added, his tone calm and supportive.

By the time Luna reached the bottom of the slope, her heart was racing, but it wasn't from fear—it was from pure joy. She had done it. And more than that, she had done it with the two men who had come to mean everything to her.

As she slowed to a stop, Kai skidded to her side, coming to a graceful halt with a dramatic spray of snow. He threw his arms up in the air and cheered. "That was amazing! See? I told you you'd nail it!"

Luna laughed, breathless but exhilarated. "I actually did it!"

Logan arrived next, his usual calm demeanor cracking just enough to let a small smile break through. "Told you you had it in you," he said, pulling her in for a quick, heated kiss before stepping back, his hand lingering on her waist.

Luna looked between the two of them, her chest swelling with happiness. This was her life now—an unconventional love with two men who saw her for who she really was, who challenged her, supported her, and made her feel like she could conquer anything.

As they stood together at the bottom of the slope, with the sun shining brightly above and the snowy mountains rising majestically behind them, Luna realized something important. Life wasn't about following the rules, or fitting into a box that others had created for her. It was about carving her own path, just as she had on the slopes today.

She had rewritten the rules of her life, and now, with Logan and Kai at her side, she was ready for whatever came next.

"Ready for round two?" Kai asked, grinning mischievously.

Luna smirked, glancing at Logan, who gave her a nod of approval. She clicked her poles into the snow, a new surge of confidence coursing through her.

"Let's do it," she said, knowing that whatever happened, she was exactly where she was meant to be.

And as they made their way back up the slope together, laughing and teasing, Luna knew that this was just the beginning of a new adventure—one filled with love, passion, and the kind of freedom she had always craved.